THE FLYING BEAVER BROTHERS AND THE MUD-SLINGING MOLES

MAXWELL EATON III

ALFRED A. KNOPF
NEW YORK

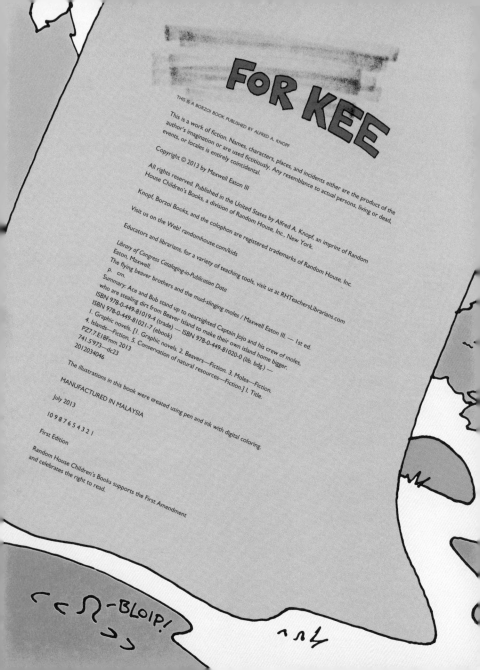

FOR KEE

THIS IS A BORZOI BOOK PUBLISHED BY ALFRED A. KNOPF

Visit us on the Web! randomhouse.com/kids

Educators and librarians, for a variety of teaching tools, visit us at RHTeachersLibrarians.com

Library of Congress Cataloging-in-Publication Data
Eaton, Maxwell.
The flying beaver brothers and the mud-slinging moles / Maxwell Eaton III. — 1st ed.
p.   cm.
Summary: Ace and Bub stand up to nearsighted Captain Jojo and his crew of moles, who are stealing dirt from Beaver Island to make their own island home bigger.
ISBN 978-0-449-81019-4 (trade) — ISBN 978-0-449-81020-0 (lib. bdg.) —
ISBN 978-0-449-81021-7 (ebook)
1. Graphic novels. [1. Graphic novels. 2. Beavers—Fiction. 3. Moles—Fiction.
4. Islands—Fiction. 5. Conservation of natural resources—Fiction.] I. Title.
PZ7.7.E18Fmm 2013
741.5'973—dc23
2012034046

The illustrations in this book were created using pen and ink with digital coloring.

MANUFACTURED IN MALAYSIA

July 2013

10 9 8 7 6 5 4 3 2 1

First Edition

WHY?

SOMETHING STRANGE IS HAPPENING. WE NEED TO TALK!

BUT OUR SHOW IS ON.

KA.

WE NEED TO TALK!

FINE. I'LL THROW DOWN THE LADDER. . . .

IT SHOULD REACH.

WHAT JUST HAPPENED?

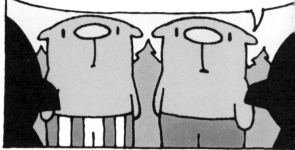

WAIT, YOU GUYS DON'T KNOW ANYTHING ABOUT THIS?

WHY WOULD WE?

WELL, THESE THINGS SEEM TO HAPPEN WHEN YOU'RE AROUND. . . .

HEY, I'D LIKE TO SEE *YOU* BUILD A FISH HOTEL WITHOUT FLOODING THE BACK OF THE ISLAND.

KA.

I THINK WE MISSED THAT ONE.

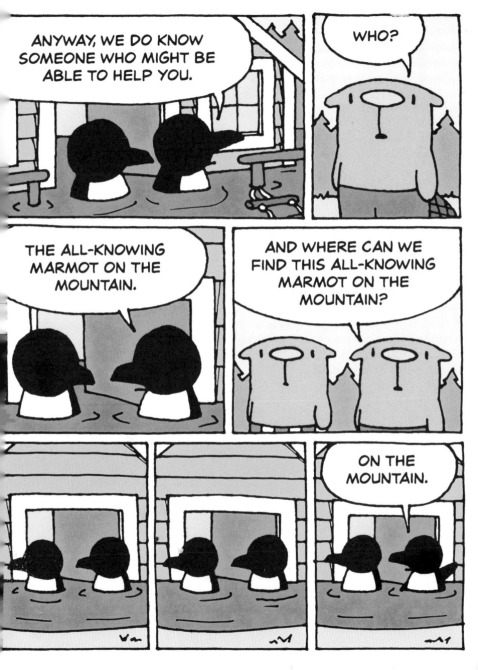

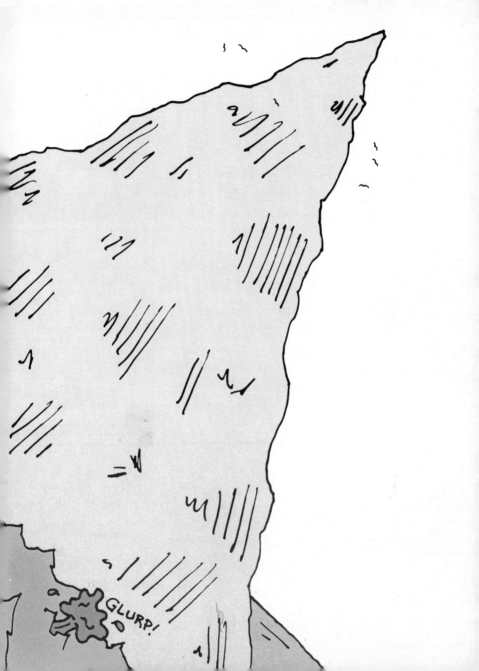

AH!

SORRY, I DON'T GET MANY VISITORS UP HERE.

EXCEPT FOR THOSE TWO PUFFINS . . .

PENGUINS.

ANYWAY, WE CAME TO ASK YOU A QUESTION.

HE THINKS HE'S SO SMART....

WE WERE HOPING YOU MIGHT KNOW WHY EVERYTHING ON THE ISLAND IS SINKING INTO THE MUD.

AND FUNNY? EVERYONE THINKS HE'S HILARIOUS, WHEN *I'M* THE FUNNY ONE!

WHOA, LOOK AT THAT!

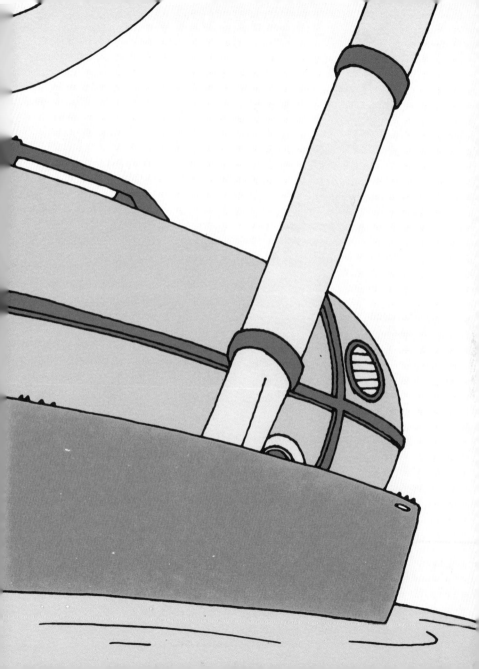

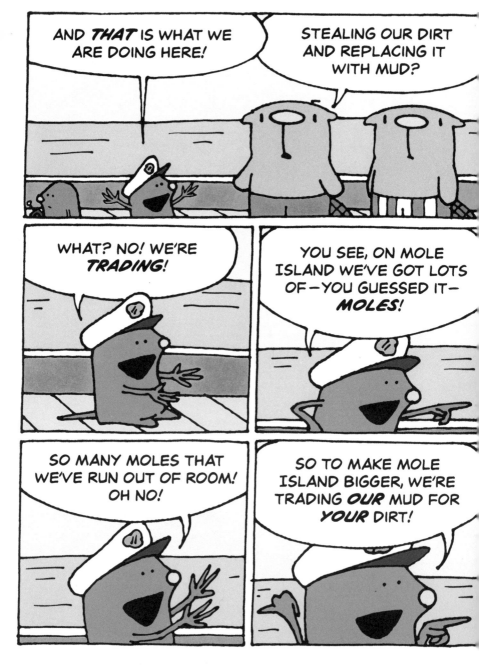

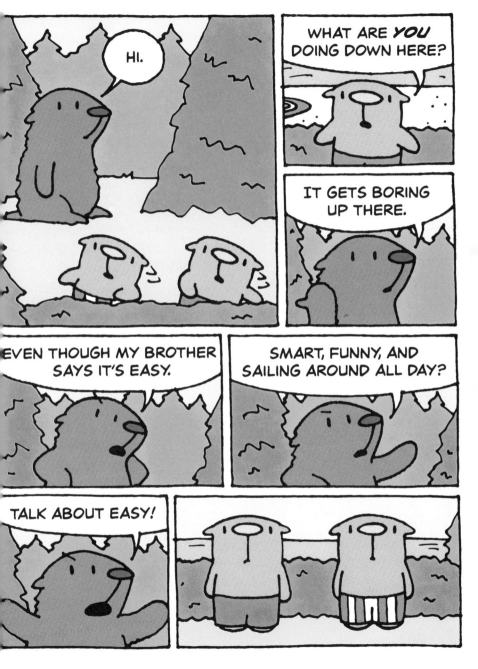

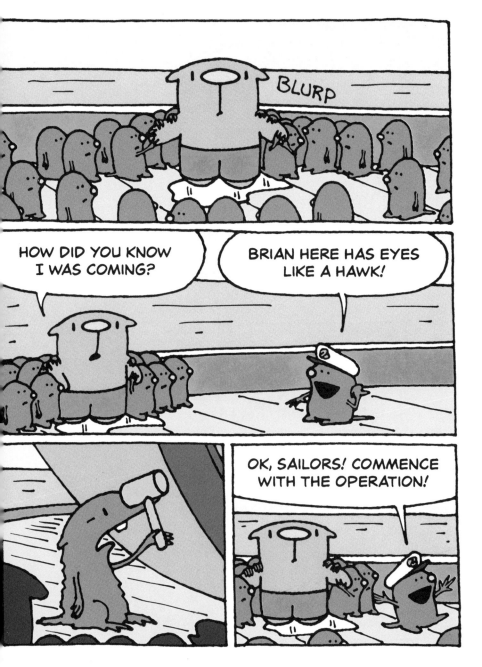

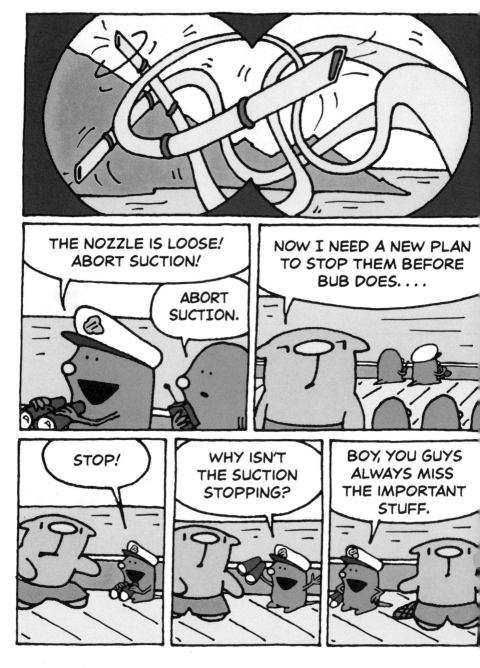

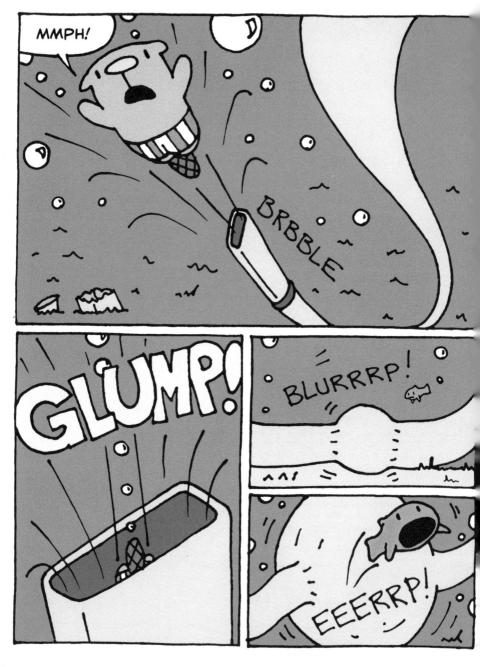

VVVVVRR
GLUG
GLUG
GLUG
GLUG
ROOSH
CUSH
PFFF!
YUT!
PSSSST!
HOLEY MOLEY
MOLE ISLAND
TSS!
SHUP!
SHUP!

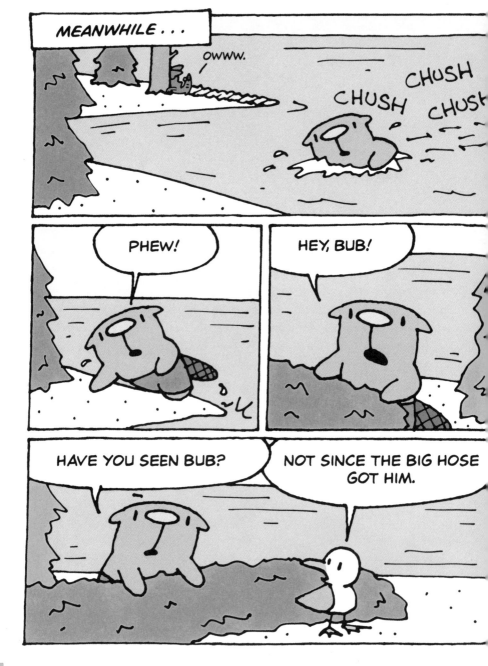

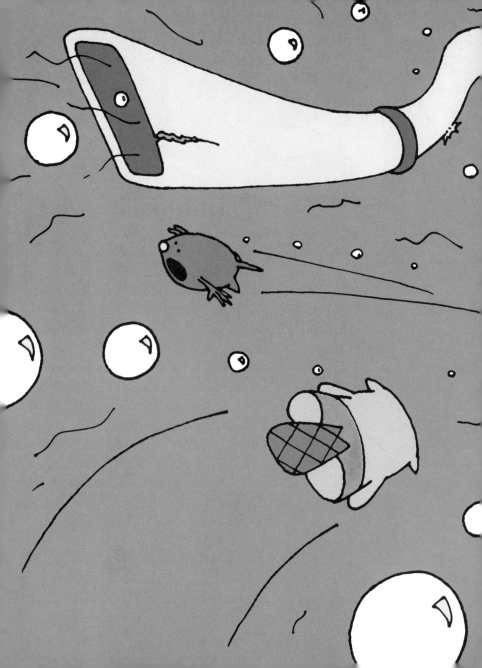

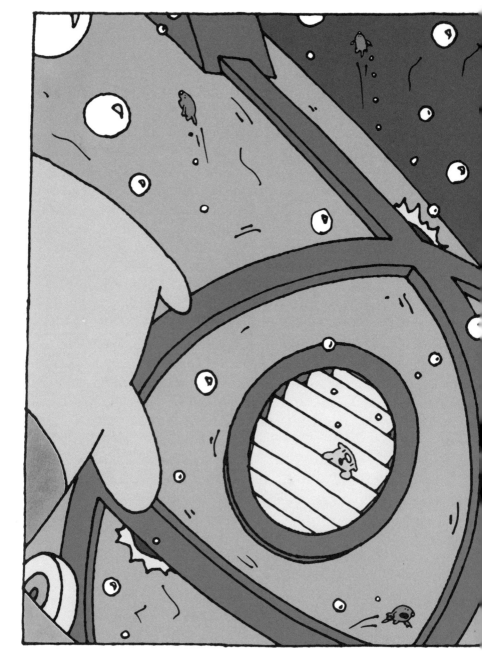